Stardust

Stardust

Jeremy Bickham

Jeremy P. Bickham

Contents

Once upon a time in the far reaches of space, a humble starship called the Quasar hovers across the starry sky. Inside the vessel are two peculiar aliens. They are a true-blue Starling named Stardust and his little yellow robotic friend called Gizmo. Together, the out-of-this-world pair have traversed the cosmos...visiting many different worlds. However, on one fateful day, Stardust and Gizmo would end up on an adventure that would change their lives like never before. It all began like any other day out in space when Stardust and Gizmo found themselves in quite a dilemma.

"Oh stars," Stardust sighed. "I think we might be lost Gizmo."

"It would seem that way," Gizmo agreed with the young Starling. "By the looks of things, we might've taken a wrong turn."

"Typical," the Starling shook his head. "Well, at least things can't get any worse."

As luck would have it, the young Starling suddenly sensed something off as he looked towards the plasma window of the Quasar.

"Uh oh," Stardust realizes. "I guess I spoke too soon."

In an instant, an unexpected comet bumped into the Quasar and caused it to spiral out of control. As the starship spun rapidly, Stardust and Gizmo were flung into the wall of the Quasar.

"If I were organic like you...," Gizmo said as he started to feel dizzy. "I would certainly feel nauseous right now."

"I can relate Gizmo," Stardust replied. "Trust me on that."

As the Quasar continued to spiral across space, a remote planet came into view. When the young Starling saw this, he made his way to the controls and managed to stop the

Quasar from heading towards it. After regaining control of the starship, Stardust and Gizmo decided to examine it for possible damage on the new planet's surface. Once they landed, the young starling and robot walked out and surveyed the Quasar.

"Well, how about that," Gizmo stated after finishing his scan. "The Quasar seems no worse for wear, so we might be able to return to space when we're ready."

"That's good to hear," Stardust smiled in relief before surveying their new surroundings. "Then again, we might have some time to explore this world before we go."

"Indeed," the little robot agreed. "This world does seem to be uncharted; we might make a few discoveries while we're here."

"Alright then," said Stardust. "Let's get exploring."

So, Stardust and Gizmo proceeded to look around this brand-new planet, with the hope of learning a bit more about this new world they were on. As they trekked across the forest, the alien duo took the time to admire the great assortment of flora and fauna all around them. But then out of nowhere, both Stardust and Gizmo were caught by surprise when they heard what sounded like singing close by.

"Well, that's peculiar," the young starling said curiously.

"I guess we're not the only advance beings in this world after all," Gizmo added. "You think it might be one of the planet's resident species."

"Only one way to find out," Stardust stated as he and Gizmo proceeded to follow the source of the singing.

The pair followed the harmonious voice across the forest until finally, Stardust and Gizmo spotted the source of the singing...coming from what appeared to be a cute and beautiful young lady of an anthropoid species. As the young woman sang, a good assortment of animals surrounded her as they listen to her beautiful voice.

"Wow," Stardust whispered in astonishment. "The residents of this world seem...amazing."

"Indeed," Gizmo added in agreement. "Especially the way those creatures are surrounding that anthropoid without showing either nervousness or hostility."

"That too," Stardust quietly replied.

The pair continued to watch the young lady secretly, while she proceeded to talk with the woodland creatures.

"Well, hello again my little friends," the young lady said sweetly. "I am so happy to have you here with me today because it won't be long before a special day will be here. Do you know the one I'm talking about?"

The creatures nodded as they chirped, squeaked, and made a great assortment of chattering within their species' tongues.

"That's right," the young lady giggled. "My 18th birthday is coming up and I'm excited, especially since my uncle told me that something special will happen on that day."

The woodland creatures cheered for the young lady as they happily embraced her, while Stardust and Gizmo continued to observe her quietly until they finally decided to head back to the Quasar.

"Perhaps we should head back to the ship before she notices," Gizmo suggested.

"Good idea," Stardust agreed with the little robot. "Let's go."

Stardust and Gizmo proceeded to depart; however, they didn't realize that the log they were standing on was starting to bend until...snap! When the log broke in two, Stardust and Gizmo crashed into the foliage while catching the maiden and her woodland friends by surprise.

"Oh my," said the young lady. "I wonder who's out there?"

Determined to find out, the young lady followed the source of the crash where to her surprise she spotted Stardust and Gizmo as they shakily got back up to their feet.

"I guess we should've checked how rotted that log was first," Stardust admitted as he brushed himself off.

"Perhaps," Gizmo replied. "Though hopefully, we haven't drawn too much..."

Just before the little robot finished his sentence, he and Stardust realized that the young maiden is now looking at them with a mixture of shock and surprise.

"Oh boy," Stardust said in disbelief at being spotted.

There was an awkward silence as the two aliens and the young lady looked at one another for a brief moment until Gizmo decided to greet the maiden.

"Greetings and salutations organic lifeform." Gizmo happily greeted the young lady.

Upon hearing the little robot talk, the young lady yelped in shock before tripping backward as she struggled to get away from the alien beings.

"Wait don't go!" said Stardust as he tries to calm the maiden down. "We're not going to hurt you!"

"Who are you two?! the young lady asks in fear and confusion. "and... what are you two?!"

"It's okay..." Stardust assures the young lady as he helped her to her feet. "My name is Stardust and this little robot here is one of my friends... Gizmo."

"It is a pleasure to meet you, Madame," Gizmo added as he offered his tendril-like front limb. "Do you have a name or designation by any chance?"

"Last time I checked, my name is Estella..." the young lady said while brushing the dust off herself. "But now I think I'm beginning to doubt my senses."

"That's quite understandable," Gizmo replied. "By the look of things, your planet doesn't seem to get many off-world visitors such as us."

"Off-world?" Estella asked in confusion. "You mean like the stars?"

"More or less," Stardust replied. "If you would like, we could take you to our ship so we could explain a bit about ourselves."

"Alright then," Estella sighed. "Though I am confused about why you would have a boat this close to the forest."

Stardust and Gizmo looked at one another before looking at Estella, who innocently smiled at the pair before waving in a friendly gesture. It became clear that the pair have their work cut out, in explaining themselves to this resident of the planet. Stardust and Gizmo manage to escort Estella to the Quasar and proceeded to show her around. Sure enough, the young maiden became astonished by what she saw within the space vessel. For it was clear that many of the things within the Quasar are far beyond anything her world has accomplished so far.

"Wow Stardust," Estella said in astonishment. "All of these things you have here are quite amazing!"

"I guess it is," the young Starling casually shrugged. "Most of these are just your every-day common technology found in type two and type three civilizations."

"I see," the young lady somewhat understood. "And I especially like this thing that lights on and off."

"You mean the lamp?" Gizmo asked the young lady who nodded in response.

After being shown around the Quasar for some time, Estella quickly remembered that she should head back home.

"I should probably get going now," Estella informed the alien beings. "I don't want my uncle to begin worrying about me."

"I guess that's understandable," said Stardust. "Take care of yourself out there, okay?"

"I will," Estella assured the young Starling before giggling. "I hope I can meet you two again real soon."

"Well....," Stardust said as he and Gizmo thought this over for a bit before finally giving the young maiden their answer. "I guess since we don't have anywhere else to go at the moment, we might be able to stay on your planet for a bit."

"That is true," Gizmo added. "So, feel free to pay a visit if you like."

"That's wonderful to hear," Estella smiled brightly. "I'll make sure to drop by after my uncle and I return from a trip into the village tomorrow afternoon."

"Then I guess we'll see you again," said Stardust. "Have a good evening."

After saying their farewell, Stardust and Gizmo watched as the young lady departed for her home.

"She's...quite a peculiar being isn't she Gizmo," said Stardust.

"She is," Gizmo nodded in response. "Well, hopefully, we'll be able to see her again in the future."

As the pair proceeded to relax from their first day in this new world, they had little idea that somewhere in outer space...a dark and foreboding vessel lurks within the starry sky. In the vessel, an even more shadowy figure looks upon the blue planet with interest as he contemplated his intention for the planet.

"At last," the hidden figure said sinisterly. "A perfect spot to begin terraforming a perfect world."

On the next day, Stardust woke up from his bed and proceeded to start his morning.

"Huh, seems like a perfect day to meditate," Stardust said as he took in the fresh air.

After eating his breakfast, taking a shower, and brushing his teeth, the young Starling proceeded to head out for his morning meditation.

"I am going to go out for a bit to meditate Gizmo," Stardust informed the little robot. "I'll see you when I get back."

"Alright Stardust," Gizmo chuckled. "I'll let you know of the progress with the data of this planet when you get back."

"Okay," the young Starling replied. "See you later."

With that said Stardust went outside to find a good spot for his meditation. He found it in the forest at a small spot, down by a small stream that flowed towards the village Estella spoke of yesterday.

Sure enough, the young Starling kneeled, close his eyes, and began his meditation. As he cleared his mind of certain unwanted thoughts, the young Starling found himself at peace. But then out of nowhere, Stardust's meditation was interrupted when he heard what sounded like a tremendous growl and the screams of multiple people.

"Huh, well so much for my meditation," Stardust groaned in disappointment as he looked in the direction of the noises. "If I didn't know any better, I'd say that this village Estella spoke of might need some help."

Determined to find out, Stardust raced towards the village to see what was the matter. When he got there, the young Starling was astonished at what he was seeing as a tremendous dragon soared over the settlement.

"Now that's something you don't see every day," Stardust said to himself. "But then again, I've seen a lot of things in this universe that you don't usually see every day anyway."

Curious as to why the reptilian creature seemed to be rampaging across the village, the young Starling decided to check it out as he began to channel blue energy around himself before taking to the air and flying up to the dragon. Baffled at seeing the Starling in the air with it, the mighty reptile examined Stardust curiously as Stardust waved at the dragon.

"Uh, hello there," Stardust greeted the dragon. "Sorry if I'm bothering you, but I'm not sure it is a good idea to frighten the humans that call this village home...do you think?"

At first, the dragon felt a bit confused about the alien being. However, the dragon decided to open its jaw to show the young Starling something. As Stardust got a good look at the mouth of the beast, he quickly understood the reason behind the dragon's rampage.

"I see now," Stardust understood. "Let's see if we can get that out for you."

Without haste, Stardust reached inside the dragon's mouth until he finally pulled out what appeared to be a broken tooth which was giving the dragon a painful toothache. Relieved at no longer feeling pain within its mighty jaws, the grateful dragon gently nuzzled the Starling in gratitude.

"You're welcome," Stardust chuckled as he pets the now docile dragon. "Now try to stay out of trouble, okay?"

The dragon nodded in understanding before flying back to its lair, while Stardust hovered back down to the ground in relief that the village is once again at peace.

"Well, that was a lot more excitement than I expected today," Stardust admitted. "But at least now I can hopefully get back to my meditation."

Just before he left, Stardust noticed as the astonished villagers looked upon the Starling in a mixture of shock and amazement that this mysterious being was able to stop the dragon's rampage until finally…they began to clap and cheer at their savior who simply scratched his head humbly at the attention he was getting. Then, the young Starling noticed as Estella was among the cheering crowd alongside an elderly gentleman who proceeded to walk up to Stardust.

"That was amazing Stardust," Estella cheered. "Thank you for stopping the dragon."

"Indeed," the gentleman added. "Very few have dared to try to soothe a dragon before, normally most would rather try and slay the beasts."

"Well, that's a little barbaric," Stardust cringed at the thought. "Most of us Starlings only believe in inflicting harm when all other options are exhausted. All life is precious and worth protecting."

"Such wise words young visitor," the gentleman chuckled. "My name is Presto and I guess you already met my niece, Estella."

"Indeed," the young lady giggled. "Though technically we're related more by heart rather than by blood."

"I see," Stardust understood.

"Anyway," Uncle Presto proceeded to say. "We have just finished our shopping for the ingredients I need for a new potion, so we should head back home my dear."

"Alright then," Estella replied. "Though hopefully, I'll see you and Gizmo later."

"Okay Estella," Stardust nodded before departing. "You two have fun with your potion thing."

When he got back to the Quasar, Stardust was finally able to meditate in peace. Afterward, there was a knock at the airlock which both Stardust and Gizmo knew was most likely their new friend Estella. Sure enough, the pair saw that the young lady brought her uncle as well for the elderly gentleman wanted to show the alien duo the new potion, he created.

"Here it is," Uncle Presto said as he showed everyone his new potion. "I think I finally got the ingredients right to transform lead into gold this time around."

"It has been his biggest project since before I started living with him," Estella replied sweetly.

"Hate to break this to everyone," Gizmo said. "But chemical reactions will never change one element into another, it can only transfer the electrons between elements...not the protons within the nucleus of the atoms that define the element in question."

"While I may not fully understand what you said my fine mechanical being, the only way to know for sure is to give it a shot," Uncle Presto chuckled.

"Well, you could at least try your little experiment...," Stardust tried to say before the man poured the potion onto the lead he brought to demonstrate. "Outside."

Once the potion was on the lead; it suddenly caused the metal to liquefy and dissolve instantly much to the gentleman's disappointment.

"Oh well," Uncle Presto sighed. "Better luck next time I guess."

"Indeed, Uncle Presto," Estella replied while she tried to hold in her laughter.

"I did try saying it wouldn't work," Gizmo shook his head. "Though at least it was a good attempt."

"For the most part," Stardust added with a chuckle. "I'm sure your potions will find their use one of these days."

"I'm certain they will," Uncle Presto chuckled. "Just not for making gold, that's for sure."

Sure enough, everyone on the starship began to laugh a bit at Uncle Presto's humor. Once the laughter ended, Stardust and Estella suddenly looked into one another's eyes. As the two gazed at one another, a strange feeling began to occur within both Stardust and Estella... as if a new kind of connection was beginning to occur. Realizing what was happening, the two blushed for a moment as the Starling and the young lady try not to think about it as they quickly regained their composure.

"I... guess we should probably head home," Estella said quietly.

"Probably a good idea my dear," Uncle Presto agreed. "Our roast boar should be ready by now."

"Well, that sounds appetizing," said Stardust.

"A lot of these Earth cuisines certainly do," Gizmo added. "Might be interesting to see if we can replicate them with the synthesizer."

"You two have a safe trip back home, okay?" Stardust said to Estella and her adoptive uncle.
    "

Thank you, Stardust," Estella smiled sweetly.

As time went by, young Estella began to spend more time with both Stardust and Gizmo. Especially when the young maiden was eager to show her new alien friends some of the things that make the Earth fascinating, such as introducing them to her animal friends in the forest. Although hesitant at first, Estella's woodland friends quickly grew to enjoy interacting with the young Starling and his robotic friend...even though Stardust found it a little awkward when the animals got comfortable around him.

"Oh stars," Stardust said as Estella's woodland friends happily settled down and rested by him. "This seems a little much isn't it?"

"Don't worry Stardust," Estella assured the young Starling. "They're just happy to have made some brand-new friends."

The next thing Estella did was to introduce Stardust to the local library, where the young Starling became astonished by the vast assortment of books in front of him.

"This is amazing Estella," Stardust said with enthusiasm. "The only form of reading material that is common these days in the galactic community is either Holo-books or eBooks, I never thought in my lifetime I'll ever see an actual printed book."

"Then I guess it was a good idea we came then," Estella giggled before noticing a book she wanted to check out from the top of the shelf. "I better go and find the ladder if I'm going to get that book down."

"Actually," the young Starling said. "I might have an idea."

Sure enough, the young Starling channeled energy around him once more as he was able to use it to summon the book toward his hand.

"Wow, Stardust!" Estella said in amazement. "That magic you're using is pretty powerful."

"What you just saw was Cosmic energy actually," Stardust corrected the young lady. "And I have a sneaky suspicion that it's at least fifty times more powerful than magic.'

"What is Cosmic Energy Stardust?" Estella wondered.

"Hm... how do I put this?" Stardust said as he tried to explain Cosmic energy to his human friend and an idea came to him. "You can think of Cosmic Energy as the energy that maintains the balance of the entire cosmos and exists everywhere within and around us."

"Whoa," Estella gasped at what she has heard. "And you can tap into this cosmic energy Stardust."

"Anyone can actually," Stardust chuckled. "All it takes is for your mind, body, and spirit to work together as one."

"I see," Estella nodded in understanding. "Thank you for helping me reach my book."

"Don't mention it," Stardust blushed while he rubbed his right arm. "It's the least I can do."

After their time at the library, Stardust and Estella proceeded to head back to their homes when they stop by one structure that stands out. It is a tremendous and luxurious palace, that stands across from the village.

"Good grief," Stardust shook his head. "Don't see the point or practicality of having a monarch, I mean all the power given to them simply just corrupts their purpose as the nobles busy themselves with playing politics and attaining more wealth for themselves."

"Well, that's a little unfair Stardust," Estella said in disappointment at what she is hearing. "Because my father is the reigning monarch of Arcadia."

"Really?!" Stardust said in surprise. "But that would make you..."

"A princess," Estella replied. "And while some of what you said may be true at times with most monarchs, my father worked with the crowned republic to make sure something like that doesn't happen."

"Oh," Stardust understood as he realized his blunder. "Huh, I am sorry about what I said, Estella. That was condescending of me to say."

"It's Alright Stardust," Estella assured the young Starling. "You had no idea and that is understandable."

As the young princess looked toward the palace, she sighs for a moment as she thinks about her father the king.

"I sure hope he is doing okay with the current quest," Estella said solemnly. "He's been gone from Arcadia for ten years now since the day he allowed me to stay with Uncle Presto until he returned."

"It'll be okay Estella," Stardust assured Estella. "I'm sure that one day, you two will be reunited soon enough."

"Thank you, Stardust," Estella smiled sweetly. "You truly are a noble being to be around. Have you...ever thought about your family where you are from Stardust."

"Actually...I haven't thought about my family in quite some time," Stardust admitted. "I haven't even thought about my home planet Astraeus until now."

"Really? Estella asked the young Starling. "Why is that, Stardust?"

"Because a while back," Stardust proceeded to say. "Astraeus was engulfed by a black hole that came out of nowhere while I was still in space, and as far as I know...I might be one of the few Starlings that remain in this universe."

As the Starling looks down solemnly, he feels Estella's hand as she places it on his shoulder. In her eyes, Stardust could see the empathy and sorrow the young princess feels over what happened to him.

"Why Stardust, I'm so sorry to hear that," Estella said as she sadly closed her eyes. "I know I would feel the same way if anything like that happened to Earth."

Stardust offered a part of his red scarf to Estella so she could wipe away her tears, which the young lady obliges as she did so.

"It's quite alright Estella," Stardust happily assures the princess. "I am no longer alone, now that I have friends like you, Gizmo, and Uncle Presto. While I might always miss Astraeus and everyone I cared about back on the planet, with all of you by my side...I no longer have to feel that I'm on my own."

"You... mean that Stardust?" Estella asks in amazement.

"You can bet on that," the young Starling happily replied.

As the two looked into one another's eyes once more, they suddenly felt that peculiar urge once more. Though this time, neither Stardust nor Estella felt embarrassed by this strange new feeling that has developed. Sure enough, the young Starling thought of an idea.

"Say, Estella," Stardust proceeded to ask. "If you are not too busy, would you like Gizmo and me to show you around space for a bit? I'm certain it will be an experience you might enjoy."

"Well Stardust," Estella said as she gave the Starling her answer. "I think I'll like that a lot."

Sure enough, Stardust and Gizmo brought Estella along as they eagerly showed her around much of outer space. From seeing brand new stars to visiting a great assortment of planets, moons, and other unique celestial bodies, Princess Estella indeed found herself enjoying this out-of-this-world adventure her new alien friends are showing her. Afterward, the Quasar landed back on Earth and Estella proceeded to head back to the cottage after such a long and incredible trip.

"That was truly the most remarkable experience I have had in my entire lifetime," Estella cheered. "Thank you for the voyage you two."

"You're welcome, Estella," Stardust smiled.

"It was the least we can do your highness," Gizmo added. "Have a safe trip back to the cottage."

"I'm certain I will," Estella giggled. "I better head to bed early after dinner when I get back, otherwise I'll be tuckered out during my birthday tomorrow."

"Indeed," Stardust agreed. "It'll be your 18th year of being born."

"Quite an achievement for your species," Gizmo said in agreement. "Especially in the culture of this part of the planet."

"That's right," Estella said before she thought of something. "Say, would you two like to attend as well? It might make my party even more wonderful if you both came to it."

"We'll...think about it," Stardust reluctantly stated. "Goodnight Estella."

"Same to you Stardust," Estella replied before pecking the young Starling on the cheek with a kiss.

With that said, the young princess departed back to the cottage while Stardust remained surprised by what Estella did.

"You seem to like her don't you Stardust?" the little robot asked curiously.

"Well, I don't know...maybe," Stardust admitted. "Though I must admit, these new feelings I'm having are still a bit confusing."

"Love can be at times," said Gizmo. "Or at least that is what I have stored in my databanks."

"Right now, I have no idea how to tell her," Stardust sighed. "Not to mention how she'll think of it when or if I do express my new feelings."

"Well, you'll never know until you try Stardust," Gizmo stated before walking inside the ship to power down and recharge. "That's all you can do."

Thinking about what his robotic companion said, Stardust proceeded to contemplate the idea of telling Estella how he felt about her and then proceeded to get some sleep before he and Gizmo head towards the cottage for the Princess's birthday. On the next day in the afternoon, there was a knock on the door of Uncle Presto's cottage. As the old gentleman answered it, there stood Stardust and Gizmo who have come to attend Estella's 18th birthday party.

"So, you two did make it after all," Uncle Presto chuckled. "My dear niece was hoping you would."

"Well, we wouldn't miss it for the universe," Stardust replied.

"It does indeed sound like a fun festivity," Gizmo added.

"Well then, come on in," Uncle Presto invited the pair. "Estella's in the other room waiting to get started.

Very soon, the party proved to be quite a fun festivity indeed as the two aliens joined their new human friends in having fun during Princess Estella's birthday. From a great assortment of party games to eating a few slices of birthday cake, Estella's 18th birthday proved to be one of the most exciting things that both Stardust and Gizmo have ever experienced. Then, something interesting happened as Uncle Presto presented the young princess with a surprise in the form of a letter.

"Happy birthday my dear," Uncle Presto smiled at his adopted niece. "Your father wanted me to give this to you on this particular day."

As Estella read the letter, her eyes widen in amazement at what it said. For it is revealed that her father, King Solaris has returned from his quest and is eager to see his beloved daughter once again real soon.

"My goodness!" Estella cheered in amazement. "This is probably...one of the best birthdays I have ever had!!! Oh, thank you, Uncle Presto, this was wonderful to hear."

"You're welcome your majesty, "Uncle Presto bowed humbly. "Maybe after the party, we can go and see your father at the palace."

"Indeed," Estella said before looking to Stardust and Gizmo. "I can't wait to introduce you to my father, I bet he'll be astonished to meet visitors from beyond the stars."

"I'm sure he will," Stardust chuckled at seeing the princess's enthusiasm. "Before we go though, would you mind if I tell you something in private?"

"I don't see why not," Estella casually shrugged. "I could use some fresh air anyway."

As the two went outside, Stardust felt nervous for a moment at the thought of telling the young princess how he felt. But he knew that sooner or later, he will have to say it.

"So, I guess this means you'll be back to living at your original home in the palace," said Stardust. "I bet it'll be quite a development for you."

"Perhaps," Estella admitted. "But of course, I will always visit Uncle Presto and all the friends I made in the village. I will even make time to visit you and Gizmo as well if that is okay with you of course."

"It is," Stardust said before gulping down a big swallow as he knew this might be the one chance, he must tell the princess. "Estella, there's something I want to tell you...though I'm not quite sure how to say it."

"What is it, Stardust?" Princess Estella wondered curiously.

Just before he had the chance to say something, the young Starling sensed something was off as he and the young princess noticed something hovering in the sky.

"Stardust, what is that thing?" Estella asked curiously.

"It... can't be," Stardust replied in disbelief. "It's a planet breaker!"

"Planet breaker," Estella gasped at hearing the name of the space station. "That doesn't sound friendly."

"That's because it isn't," Stardust said sternly. "Planet breakers are created specifically to alter a celestial body into a more suitable world, but the effects they have can be detrimental to the life that already resides there."

"Oh no," Estella gasped fearfully. "We have to do something to stop that thing before everyone on Earth perishes."

"I know," Stardust agreed with the young lady. "Though we have to figure out how."

As they thought about the dire situation in front of them, Stardust suddenly thought of an idea.

"Say, Estella," the young Starling wondered. "Does your uncle still have that potion he was using to make gold?"

"Why of course," Estella replied. "He placed it with his other failed potions, why do you ask."

"Because I have a feeling that we'll need something that can dissolve the core of a planet breaker," Stardust explained as he looked towards the malicious station. "Especially since we're going up there to stop it for good."

After Stardust explained his plan to Estella, Gizmo, and Uncle Presto, the four got on board the Quasar and flew up towards the station to destroy the planet breaker.

"Alright Gizmo," Stardust informed his robotic companion. "Warp us in."

"Will do," Gizmo replied nervously. "Just be careful while you're onboard that station."

"We'll try our best Gizmo," Stardust assured the little robot.

With that said, the little robot warped the Starling and the two humans onboard the planet breaker. Within the station, the three looked on in disdain at the foreboding sight of the place inside but they continue onward to find the core. Sure enough, Estella spotted what they were looking for.

"I think I found the core," Estella gestured to Stardust and her adoptive uncle.

"Good eye Estella," Stardust said while the young princess smiled. "Now let's see if the potion will work this time."

"I'm certain it will," Uncle Presto replied as he readied the potion. "If it dissolved the lead I was going to turn into gold, it should be able to destroy this contraption easily."

Just before the alchemist could pour the potion onto the core, however...

"I wouldn't do that if I were you three," a voice called out catching everyone by surprise.

As they turned around, Stardust, Estella, and Uncle Presto found themselves face-to-face with the vile owner of the station.

"Is that...another Starling like you Stardust?" Estella asked her alien friend in disbelief.

"It is," Stardust solemnly replied. "But he's not just any Starling, he's... Erebus!"

"Aw, so I see that some Starlings still recognize who I am," the dark Starling said with a sinister chuckle. "Even after being exiled by the long-gone planet for over a millennium."

"How could anyone forget about Erebus the Tyrant," Stardust solemnly said. "A rogue Starling that committed tremendous crimes across the universe, such as eradicating or enslaving countless species in a ceaseless zealous quest for conquest."

"Oh, my," Estella gasped over what was said. "And now he's trying to eradicate us, just so he could conquer Earth."

"In a way," Erebus calmly replied. "Though I consider this as more of a chance to bring our species back to glory, by presenting a new home for any other Starlings that remain."

"But that goes completely against everything we stand for back on Astraeus!" Stardust said angrily at the tyrant. "We Starlings have always tried to promote peace, freedom, justice, and democracy across the cosmos."

"Yet look at what it brought us," Erebus chuckled sinisterly. "No home planet to go back to, no legacy to call our own now. In these dark times, we must attain whatever power we can to survive...even if it means that the weak perish so that the strong can persist."

"Only a true monster deals in such absolutes," Stardust calmly said as he pulled out and ignited his Enersword. "I'm going to put a stop to this madness, one way or the other."

"I would like to see you try," Erebus said venomously as he pulled out his Enersword and ignited it.

In an instant, Stardust and Erebus locked energy blades as their duel for the Earth's fate has begun. As each combatant swung their Enerswords, both Starlings manage to block one another's attacks. Using his eons of experience in swordsmanship and the use of Cosmic energy, Erebus was able to surprise Stardust with his dark and powerful techniques. However, Stardust uses his skills to match the seasoned tyrant while giving Estella and her uncle enough time to apply the potion to the core.

"WHAT?!!" Erebus said in disbelief as the core dissolved, causing the planet breaker to have a meltdown. "I should've known you and those anthropoids would try something during our battle."

Stardust simply gave the tyrannical Starling a smirk before calling for Gizmo to warp them back into the Quasar...leaving Erebus to growl in blinded rage while the planet breaker began to break apart until it at last imploded. With the planet breaker finally destroyed, the Quasar landed by the cottage while everyone onboard sighed in relief that the situation was over.... or so they thought. When Stardust sensed that the danger has yet to pass, he and his friends looked up in disbelief as they saw that Erebus survived the implosion and is now channeling his dark cosmic energy into a tremendous sphere.

"I must admit, that was quite a clever plan young one," Erebus laughed manically. "But now you and the inhabitants of this world have only just sealed your fate...NOW PERISH WITH THIS PLANET!!!!"

With that said, Erebus unleashed his sphere with the intent of wiping out the Earth and its inhabitants."

"Oh dear," Uncle Presto said in disbelief. "What do you propose we do now."

"I'm not sure," Stardust admitted. "I never considered our species' natural resiliency. Right now, I have no idea of what we can do to save the Earth."

"Listen to me Stardust," Estella proceeded to say. "Ever since I got to know you, I have seen you do things that even I could not imagine were possible. If there is anyone, I know who can do the impossible...I know for a fact that it is you, Stardust."

"She is correct," Gizmo added. "I for one have witnessed you pull off plenty of surprising things Stardust, so I am certain that you might be able to pull off another surprise."

Touched by what his friends have said, Stardust suddenly thought of an idea.

"Stand back everyone," Stardust informed his friends. "I'm about to try something that should be able to stop Erebus this time."

Everyone did as Stardust said, while the young Starling formed a semi-circle with his arms before he began to cup his palms. He brought them to his left side and squatted his legs a bit before reciting his most powerful technique.

"Cos... mic...!" Stardust said as his muscles tensed while small blue particles began to form into an orb within his cupped palms. "R... age...!"

When Erebus's sphere of doom came closer to the planet, Stardust knew it was time to unleash his attack.

"FURY!!!!!!" the young Starling roared out as he thrust his arms forward while the blue orb of cosmic energy blasted out and took on the form of a brilliant beam.

"IMPOSSIBLE!!!" Erebus said in disbelief as the blue beam collided with his dark sphere. "THAT CAN'T BE POSSIBLE!"

Sure enough, Stardust's Cosmic Rage Fury wave overtook Erebus's attack and struck the tyrant just before he could evade it. In an instant, the evil Starling was flung straight into space with the hope that his brief reign of terror has come to an end. Relieved that it was finally over, Stardust let out a great sigh as he came to his knee panting from near exhaustion after unleashing such a powerful technique.

"Stardust, are you Alright?" Estella asked the Starling.

"I'll be fine," Stardust assured the young princess. "Just haven't got used to using the Cosmic Rage Fury technique that's all."

"Oh, that's wonderful to hear," Estella sighed in relief. "Though I am still curious about what were you going to say before we went off to save the Earth from the tyrant from the stars."

"Well, it's a little difficult for me to tell you this Estella," Stardust sighed as he proceeded to finally say his confession. "But the truth is that...I... I love you."

"You mean it, Stardust?" Estella asked in astonishment.

The young Starling simply nodded in response, as the young princess smiled sweetly at Stardust, and then they shared a passionate kiss.

As time went on, Stardust and Estella's love continued to grow...especially after the young princess introduced the young alien to her father King Solaris. While her father was a bit surprised by this revelation, he quickly learned to accept the young Starling as part of his and Estella's life which made Stardust, his beloved princess, and even Gizmo very happy.

"You know... I do like happy endings," Gizmo joyfully stated.

"So do I Gizmo," Stardust chuckled with his robotic companion. "So do I."

Then on one faithful day, Stardust and Princess Estella said their vows and were finally married. As they and their friends looked on happily at the out-of-this-world union, Stardust and Princess Estella knew well that they would go on to live happily ever after.

The End.

Jeremy Bickham is a children's writer and illustrator from Bay City, Michigan. Diagnosed with autism at an early age, Jeremy Bickham found it quite difficult interacting with everyone and everything around him. But with the help of his family, mentors and beloved dogs, Jeremy Bickham has not only learned to over come his disability...but now strives to share his love of storytelling with everyone around him.